My Pup

by **Margaret O'Hair**

illustrated by **Tammie Lyon**

Marshall Cavendish Children

Marshall Cavendish Corporation,
99 White Plains Road, Tarrytown, NY 10591
www.marshallcavendish.us/kids

Library of Congress Cataloging-in-Publication Data
O'Hair, Margaret.
My pup / by Margaret O'Hair; illustrated by Tammie Lyon.—1st ed.
p. cm.
Summary: Brief rhyming text and illustrations show a puppy's activities,
from having a bath to eating, playing, and going for a walk.
ISBN 978-0-7614-5389-5
[1. Dogs—Fiction. 2. Animals—Infancy—Fiction. 3. Stories in rhyme.]
I. Lyon, Tammie, ill. II. Title.
PZ8.3.O353My 2008
[E]—dc22
2007011719

The text of this book is set in Century Schoolbook.
The illustrations are rendered in gouache and color pencil.
Book design by Vera Soki
Editor: Margery Cuyler

Printed in Malaysia
First edition
1 3 5 6 4 2

mc **Marshall Cavendish**
Children

To my daughter, Stephanie, and her black Labrador Retriever,
Tucker, who inspired this story!
—M.O'H.

For the Black Hoof Gang—
Ceasar Augustus Catulus Lyon, Sydney Margaret Hardoerfer,
and Cooper Wayne Hardoerfer—
thanks for all the great walks!
—T.L.

New puppy,
young puppy,
soft puppy,
small.

Grow, puppy,
run, puppy,
chase, puppy,
ball.

Hose puppy,
dirt puppy,
mud puppy,
pie.

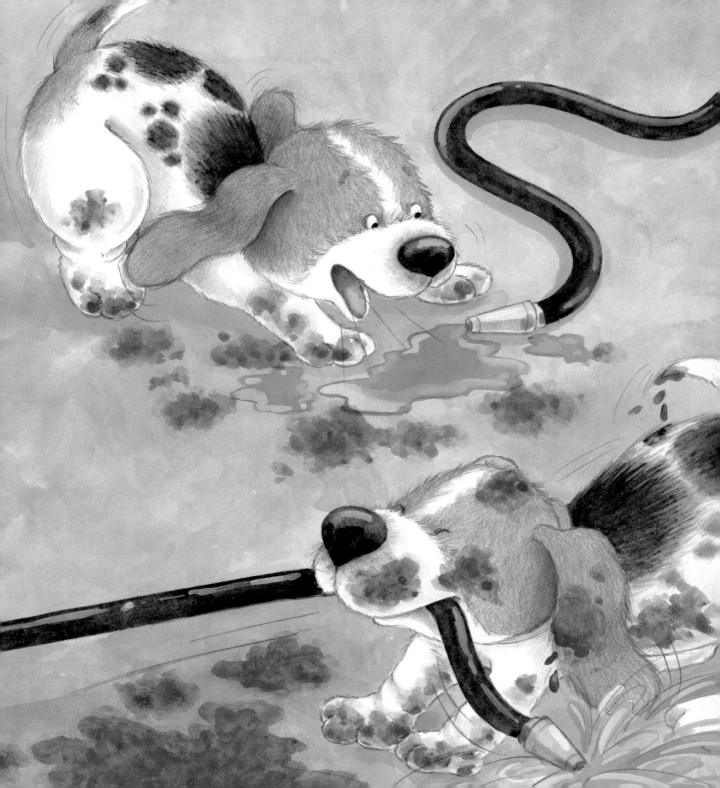

Spray puppy,
wash puppy,
towel puppy,
dry.

Crunch, puppy,
chew, puppy,
yum, puppy,
chow.

Hiss, puppy,
scratch, puppy,
poor puppy,
yowwww!

Leash puppy,
go, puppy,
yay, puppy,
walk.

Bow, puppy,
wow, puppy,
yap, puppy,
talk.

Roll, puppy,
run, puppy,
fetch, puppy,
sticks.

Paw, puppy,
shake, puppy,
smart puppy,
tricks.

Here, puppy,
come, puppy,
in, puppy,
leap.

Sit, puppy,
ride, puppy,
wind, puppy,
jeep.

Home, puppy,
stretch, puppy,
yawn, puppy,
up.

Stay, puppy,
soft puppy,
my puppy,

PUP!